Looking For The Reader

An Anthology

by

Perton Writers

CONTENTS:

I Remember When	*Peter James*
The Key To It All	*Julia Jordan*
Ghost Of Bridgnorth	*Karen Marley*
Baschurch	*Tina Bond*

Fantasy

Where The Lost Things Are	*Julie Gorman*
Leave The Weeds Alone!	*Ann Bickley*
The Symbol	*Graham Peebles*
The Gods	*Tina Bond*
Monokeros	*Julia Jordan*

What's Going On

I'm On The Run!	*Kitt Ballinger*
The Cardigan	*Ann Bickley*
Julia And Kate; *A Cautionary Tale*	*Graham Peebles*
The Golden Dragon *Haiku*	*Julie Gorman*
Bike *Haiku*	*Peter James*
The Islands Call	*Gwen Whitaker*
The Blank Card Drawer	*Dany Drummond*
It Tolls For She	*David Morgans*
Impressions Of Tequisquiapan	*Julia Jordan*

Humour

From A Cat's Perspective	*Ann Bickley*
Parrot	*David Sanders*
Eggs For Sale	*David Sanders*
Sammy The Snake	*David Sanders*
Trouble	*Julie Gorman*
Eulogy For A Sandwich	*Graham Peebles*
This Is The Life	*Tina Bond*
Two-Way Conversation	*Kitt Ballinger*

Looking For The Reader

Tuesdays

Today in the library, you'll find
Some people who are of like mind
They scribble and think
Till they run out of ink
They really are ten of a kind

Kitt Ballinger

~ All Things Spooky ~

Halloween

Upon blades of grass
Moonlight the shadow maker
Lighting up the world

Julie Gorman

Werewolf

A shining bloated moon
Heart drumming, eyes flash and flame
Hunger burns deep within

Julie Gorman

Horror Story?

In an empty room strips of thick translucent plastic hung down from the low ceiling, creating a seemingly impenetrable cave. Phosphorescent light glowed green in the dark. Strange noises could be heard chattering and clattering from within.

Something had been released, liberated, set free! The dangling bands shivered and quivered, a fearful entity began to emerge from the pitch black depths. A ghastly white face loomed from within, peering sightlessly through the curtain. There was a flailing and thrashing of limbs as it struggled to break through to the outside world.

Was it able to succeed? Could it glide through the moving strips? What horrors might follow such a terrifying monster? Might untold beings burst forth, winged and horrid, rushing unbidden into our human domain? Suddenly, as if at a sign, an icy draft blew, accompanied by a shrill whistling sound from within the opaque darkness. The creature, whatever it was moved jerkily forward. Suddenly a desperate voice cried out loudly as in a wilderness and the words were crystal clear.

'For goodness' sake mum, come out of that art installation. You've been in there long enough. They're about to close the gallery!'

Julia Jordan

A Grim Discovery

It is strange how an ordinary Sunday morning ramble turned out to be something totally unexpected. As we made our way along the muddy path that wound its way through Cardinal's Forest, I was silently cursing the fine rain which had descended upon our group of ramblers. It was the kind of rain that wasn't heavy, but nonetheless would soak through several layers of clothing and chill you to the bone; especially if you weren't wearing some form of weatherproof clothing.

With my hood up and my head down I led our intrepid little group of walkers along the path until I caught a glimpse of a brown leather boot protruding poignantly from the undergrowth. For some unknown reason a photograph from a national newspaper came to mind.

The article had been about a member of parliament who had gone missing some nine months earlier and despite several searches of his known haunts, he still had not been found.

Sir Phillip Carey-Stephenson was arguably one of the countries most hated and despised politicians, well… at least by the working classes at any rate. His stance on hiking up taxes and cutting benefits to the vulnerable made his name an anathema across all parties except for his ex-public school cronies. I immediately put up my hand and called for the group to halt. Stepping gingerly over to the partial moss covered boot; I carefully prodded at it with my walking stick, dislodging it slightly as I did so. To my utter shock and horror I saw that there was a foot and leg bone still attached to it, still covered partly in corduroy cloth and what I could only surmise was part of the owner's trousers. Some members of our rambling group began to retch and vomit whilst others, included myself could only look on morbidly.

Harry Bingham pulled out his mobile phone and said, 'Hang on folks, I'm going to call the police.' As he was busy dialling, I skirted around the rotten, offending limb, parting the dense undergrowth with my walking stick once more. After I had stepped some twenty yards I came upon more rotting and half-eaten remains. The trunk and head were lying face down on the ground, but even then, it was quite obvious to me that the body was that of a male.

I shouted to the other ramblers, 'Don't come any closer folks, I've found the rest of him here.'

'The police are on their way now mate,' Harry replied at once, 'they'll be here in five minutes.' Again the newspaper image of Sir Phillip Carey-Stephenson sprang to mind, and I somehow knew deep down, that this was him lying face down in front of me; heartless bastard that he was. I stared down at his corpse in horrible fascination and saw the hatchet sticking out obscenely from his back. It had been driven in with force. Despite the body being disturbed and eaten by carrion and rats, the axe was firmly wedged into the spine. I almost fainted in horror when I saw two familiar initials carved into its wooden handle. The axe belonged to me!

Graham Peebles

All Hallows' Eve

It was very early one dark, misty morning in October, well before the sun was up, when a man appeared from out of a side road. He was walking rapidly in the same direction along the lane leading towards the local train station. I watched him absent-mindedly as he moved through the darkness ahead of me.

Gradually the sound of his footsteps turned into distant echoes of my own and I pressed onwards hoping to be in good time for my six o'clock train.

All around me, I could feel the damp air enshrouding me in thick, dense moisture. My breath was as if vaped from the very depths of my lungs, spreading out in front of my face, a small cloud suspended in the air.

Trees by the side of the road shivered as droplets of cold water fell from sodden twigs. Old catkins and leaves hung motionless from branches. The tree trunks loomed in the gloom like nebulous giants. Somehow my usual daytime route had been transformed into the unfamiliar and I could scarcely recognize houses, drives and gardens hidden by the dank fog.

At first sight the whole world appeared to be in monotonous monochrome but as I looked up I perceived the street lamps with their luminous orange glow. They were refracting the light through the water vapour and creating an aura around each one.

On the gritty tarmac, puddles of rainbow colours gleamed in dull reflections. By now the man had vanished out of sight, and I was struck immediately by the atmosphere of absolute stillness and quiet. Then the realization dawned on me that I was not alone in experiencing this. Some nocturnal creature also felt the same and emboldened by the tranquillity began its song.

The sound flowed through the air, at first high-pitched, then descending, now quick, now slow. The robin rippled and trilled its melody, calling across the dark void.

I quickened my pace and hurried towards the iron steps leading up to the railway bridge. Climbing two steps at a time and gasping for breath I reached the top and peered over the side at the apparently deserted platform. Down the next flight of stairs I finally walked out onto the platform and felt relieved that the first part of my journey had been achieved. I prepared to settle down and wait for my train.

Suddenly the man I'd seen earlier slipped unwelcome out of the shadows. His face was hauntingly pale and drawn under the station lights, his coat pulled tightly round him. I could sense there was something strange about his appearance and I felt apprehensive as he started to make a move towards me. This was to be the beginning of my horrific nightmare.

Julia Jordan

To You My Ghost

I'm waiting patiently here all on my own, waiting just to see you one more time. Standing here at the foot of spiral stairs, I'm willing you to come. I think now at last I can see you beginning to form, a grey mist shuddering within the darkness of the moon held hours. You're becoming more sublime with each passing moment, a creation allowing a human guise to perfect itself.

Am I witnessing the genesis of a being or the re-emergence of long dead memories refusing to depart this world. I cannot avert my gaze as to what is unfolding before me. How you take each step so lightly and easily, capturing me totally with your presence. I wonder, are you here to take my soul?

Coming down the staircase towards me, I see a small smile resting on your lips but a smile that is not echoed within the darkness of your eyes. And yet you hold my stare, not willing to let it go. I cannot move.

Nearer you come, getting closer and closer. I can feel a strange power lingering amongst the air. I cannot take a breath. You're getting far to close now, but a sudden realisation whispers in my ear. You cannot see me. You do not know I am here.

Tina Bond.

~ Seasonal ~

Yuletide

Snow clad ivy sparkling and glistening
Forming patterns on red brick walls
Cobwebs frozen, stiff and unbending
Spiders now no longer tending.

Once tall trees upright and proud
Now heavy with snow, heads hung low
Branches frozen in sad drooping pose
Slow agonised death, roots frozen in snow.

Fir trees bending in sad monster shapes
Umbrella tree shelters the bushes below
Bare branches like arms desperately waving
Skies dark, and heavily laden with snow.

Tracks quickly filling as darkness creeps in
Soft snow is drifting and the wind roars
Yuletide lights flicker, brightly shining
And still the snow falls on windows and doors.

Gwen Whitaker.

We're Going to Catch Santa

We're going to catch Santa
My brother Georgie and me
When he creeps into our bedroom
All quiet, and shadowy.

He does it every year you know
It's driving us both mad, you see
He's a crafty beggar is Santa, because he knows
When were asleep.

We hang our stockings on the mantel piece
Leave him a mince pie and a tot of rum
And as we sit in front of our roaring fire
We wonder how Santa never burns his bum.

Oh, how he must huff and puff with
That great big heavy sack
When he struggles down our chimney
It's a wonder he don't wake Mum and Dad.

'Be quiet boys and go to sleep
Or he won't come!' says our Dad
'Santa doesn't come to them that's been naughty
Nor to them, that's been bad'.

So we lie awake for ages
All warm and snug in bed
Listening for the sound of his jingling bells
On the roof-top, above our head.

Now Georgie, he's fast asleep
I can hear him gently snore
But what's that creaking sound I hear?
Why, it's the opening of our door.

I've got you now I smile to myself
As I stare through a half-closed eye
There he is with his back to me
All dressed in red and white.

Shall I get him now, I wonder?
But I hold myself in check
As I hear the rustle of parcels and things
Placed gently by my bed.

I hold my breath, and take a crafty peep
Santa's torch, it slowly flickers
As he steps out, I suddenly see
That he's wearing our dad's slippers!

Graham Peebles

Two Yuletide Haiku's

Yuletide

Candles flickering
Thickest curtains tightly drawn
Smoky wood fire cracks

Julie Gorman

Sweet red wine breathing
Blanket snug upon your lap
Dog eared book awaits

Julie Gorman

Christmas Carols

Today carols are seen as part of a church tradition, but they started life long before this, as songs to celebrate various seasons of the year, including midwinter. Music prompted dancing, and by the twelfth century circle dances, 'caroles', became popular giving their name to the songs. Some of these early carols celebrated life in all its fullness and were definitely not church material. Others, such as 'The Holly and the Ivy,' and 'God Bless You Merry Gentleman,' are what we would now call folk carols.

Nonconformists embraced the music current in the eighteenth and nineteenth centuries. Charles Wesley drew on Handel's music, but he was not averse to setting his new hymns to secular tunes. Other tunes were composed to accompany hymns and psalms and have now become part of a secular tradition. 'While Shepherds Watched' was once sung to a tune called Cranbrook (1805), to which we now sing On Ilkley Moor Bah T'at.

The Church of England on the other hand was on a different course. Reluctantly, the church had provided local musicians and singers with a gallery at the west end of the church from whence they led the singing down paths many a vicar would rather not have travelled. By the middle of the nineteenth century moves were afoot to bring these free spirits into line. The introduction of Hymns Ancient and Modern in 1861 was the death knell for West Gallery Choirs. Reverential choral singing was the order of day accompanied by the organ. The West Gallery Choirs were no more.

Order had been restored but at a cost. The appeal of the new music was no match for that which it replaced, and if the church thought it was going to silence the West Gallery Choirs, it couldn't have been more wrong.

Christmas Eve was the start of Christmas celebrations, and in churches there was an atmosphere of reverence as vigils were held. Outside churches carols were sung as they had been from time immemorial; taken from house to house by groups of singers, sung in the streets, and as shocking as it may have been for those in church, carols could be heard coming from the local pub.

The church took note. Alarmed at the amount of alcohol being consumed on Christmas Eve (and no doubt the loss of the congregation as well), the Bishop of Truro had an idea for a Christmas Eve carol service within churches. The first Festival of Nine Lessons and Carols was held in 1876, and it is still one of the most popular church services today.

It was a stroke of genius on the Bishop's part to re-home carols in church, and a new Christmas tradition was born. However, successful as carol services are, they have replaced the more informal carol singing within our communities. The link with our more distant past has been broken.

Jane Smith

You Are My Hero

You are my Hero
Don't you get me
I get you
You are a breath of fresh air
With your cheeky ways
And your dark curly hair
I love your dedicated nature
And stacks of skills
Collecting and fetching
O'er dales and hills
Your selfless journeys
Back and fro... you are my hero
Its Summertime you like the best
At your behest
Let's raise a glass or two
To the sound of Summer
To our welcome guest
In the yellow and black stripy vest.

Ann Bickley

I See It All

Erect and tall
The Maypole stands
The ribbons call
I see it all!

Children playing
Bells are ringing
Ribbons waving
I see it all!

Smiling laughter
Holding ribbons
Running faster
I see it all!

Dance in the sun
Hold on! Hold on!
It's so much fun
I see it all!

Finding places
Weaving, winding
Happy faces
I see it all!

Gwen Whitaker

A Late Winter Walk

I leave my lodgings quietly so as not to disturb my fellow boarders. All I need is with me, double-checked then checked again, before closing the big old door in a special way, so the hinges wouldn't squeak.

I'm travelling light, trying to walk quietly in my three-inch stilettos. I tip-toe down the wide steps: steps that are usually heaving with young people, all in a rush. It's strange being the only person here, the whole street is deserted and very dark. It's so cold my feet are frozen already. Running past 'The Brown Cow' pub, strangely quiet and dark, I wish I'd worn boots instead of these silly shoes, but I wanted to look nice. Passing the bus depot I'm surprised at how peaceful and dark it is. It's far too early for the first drivers to be pulling out and the mechanics and cleaners would have finished all that was necessary, before one a.m.

Usually this place is a hive of activity, with engines revving, voices calling and lots of laughter and whistling. Also lots of light, from within the building and from headlights as the buses start to leave. The conductor would not switch on the internal lights until they approached their first bus stop. Soon I'll be at St. Georges. A pedestrian passage runs between the church and the Abattoir, a dark, smelly place. No lights here and the grave-stones look menacing in pre-dawn light. It's a shortcut to the station, but I'm hesitating. All I can see is a few early snow drops poking through the bushes that line the pathway. Shall I chance that there is no one lurking or shall I go the long way round where there is street lighting.

I can't risk missing the train. Off come the stilettos and I run at full pelt, holding my breath and ignoring the pain in my already frozen feet. Safely through I check the time. Must dash, I have to buy a ticket first. There isn't a soul about. No lights show in the rows of terraced houses. Not even a cat returning from its night-time hunting.

I arrive, breathless, at High Level Station. A sleepy Ticket Office Attendant looks at me suspiciously. "Trying to avoid the crush or running away from something", he said, as he pushed my ticket through the small space at the bottom of a thick, glass, arched partition. Pretending not to have heard, I gave him the money and waited impatiently for a few pennies change. It was so quiet, really spooky. Like the bus depot, this area was usually a hive of activity.

I needed to get to Low Level Station, so quickly exited the ticket office building and headed for the steep steps that led down towards it, my shoes echoing in the enclosed stairway.

At the lower level, in all directions, high walls and footpaths were made from blue bricks, which in turn were coated in black soot, so the darkness was extreme. It was eerie being the only person there. Turning right at the bottom of the steps, I could see the station and hear the train thundering along in the distance. I had to run down a zig-zag path before coming to the entrance, must hurry. If the engine driver saw an empty platform he may not stop.

The familiar chug, chug, chugging sound, hissing steam, puffing smoke and the squeal of brakes, became louder as the train slowed down. No staff on duty here, so I put a penny in the turnstile in order to get through to the platform. I looked anxiously both ways, but I was the only one there. I felt really nervous, wondering if I'd made a mistake.

As the train came to a halt, the dim lights inside the carriages beckoned to me. I pressed down the handle of the nearest carriage and climbed into the warmth. Relief flooded through me. I winced as the circulation returned to my frozen feet. A whistle blew, a flag waved and the guard stepped back into the guards-van at the rear of the train. With a jolt, a chug and the slow click of wheels on the tracks, we began to move. This was a 'no corridor' train, and I was startled to see a breathless man, running alongside, trying to open the door of my compartment. He hurled himself in and collapsed onto the bench seat opposite. We were really picking up speed now, and I was stuck with him. The next station was an hour away. Heart pounding I looked anxiously towards him. He slowly left his seat and sat very close to me. "Did you think I wouldn't come?" he asked. "My friends said you wouldn't" I answered. I can't tell you what happened next except that we were heading for Gretna Green.

Kitt Ballinger

The Merry Month of May

Bring forth the May Queen
Heralding the summertime
And the warmth of the Sun
Rejoice at the longer days and shorter nights.

Hail the children dancing
Weaving the flowery May Day vine
As around the maypole they dance
Moving step-in-step, in time.

The mayfly flutters gently
Hovering here and there
To tempt the brown trout rising
And the promise of a patiently caught supper.

New growth of plants and flower
Burst forth eager for the sunlight
Opening to its warmth
Their petals a rainbow of iridescence.

An occasional shower of rain
Refreshing and welcome
By all things that grow
But watch out for an unexpected frost!

May, one of favourite times of the year
Full of expectation and hope
Full of promise for what lies ahead
Bountiful and plenty.

Graham Peebles

Seasonal Tanka's... Japanese short poems.

Winter Tanka's

Cold frosty morning

Walking round to the station

Icy crystals there

White cobwebs draped over leaves

Winter breath appears

See the winter snow

Tramping feet try keeping warm

Hear lone robins tweet

Crispy damp leaves on the floor

Do you feel its grip?

On my way to work

Early cold winters morning

Time to see... really listen

Gnarly old oak in winter dressed

Bare branches bereft

Hiding animals

Tucked up bravely warm and snug

Nuts are stored beneath

 Do not disturb until spring

Sun and banquet time

Ann Bickley

Thwarted by Snow

Today I'm sorting through my purse
There's not much there, but what is worse
A birthday voucher, near expiry
Forgot to put it in my diary.

I've got three days, must not delay
No, only two, can't go today
They've forecast snow, with more to follow
They're always wrong, I'll go tomorrow.

Forecast was right, it snowed all night
It's minus two, what shall I do
The bus stop isn't far away
I have no choice, must go today.

The only footprints I can see
Are mine, how stupid can I be
I'm cold, it's quiet, no one to care
The bus sails past and leaves me there.

Last day, it's M&S or bust
I've got to get there, really must
I'll dress up warm and take my brolly
And my little shopping trolley.

A light bulb moment, I can go
Town isn't very far
I'll take my time, get organised

And use my battered old car.

Scraped off the snow, ready to go
Another shock, a frozen lock!
I deal with that and the battery's flat.

A sorry ending as you see
No birthday voucher gift for me
I should be crying, but let's make merry
Bring out the cream cakes and the sherry.

Thwarted by deep snow, all around
And the voucher's value?
Fifty pounds.

Kitt Ballinger

The Tears Of Autumn

A lonely tear, drifts so silently upon a cloud of dreams
Childhood wishes fall unto a quiet still heart
Raindrops no longer moisten nature's breath
Autumn weeps, for her springtime's forced to part

Shadows of winter hide what was once only sun
Memories live, deeply within winds shared together
Blossoms of the summer, never will they come
Lingering in the hour, your eyes closed forever.

Tina Bond

~ Historical ~

What Did The Romans Ever Do For Us?

What did the Romans do for us?
With other very useful things they brought the Roman
snail with their rasping grasping greedy teeth,
devouring every luscious leaf and succulent green plant I
don't like snails.

Now they're rampaging our green and pleasant
land encouraged by flooding and ever-increasing boggy
places with wet and damp winters. They have already
overrun my garden.

Last year I had the most beautiful Dahlia, a Georgia
O'Keefe type... a work of art with rosy pink hues and frills.
Pale orange inner petals and scarlet corona. It lasted ONE
night. The next day it was reduced to a soggy slimy stump.
I couldn't believe it!
So vibrant and exquisite yesterday and bitten down into
oblivion overnight. I had a murderous red haze descend. I
don't like using chemicals but have made an exception for
my Hostas now.

Some people eat snails... that's just as bad.
I just couldn't bear to chomp down on that rubbery
squashy foot, even if they do taste of mushrooms or
chicken in the Roman kitchen.

Ann Bickley

A Jacobite Am I

I am from beyond Hadrian's Wall. The tartan is what I wear and a dirk is what I carry. When the English come I shall be there, a Jacobite am I.

The weather is what I have to bear in this damp and inhospitable clime. The cold freezes your bones and anger becomes your red-hot fire. I am impatient for the battle to begin, and I load my musket.

Hunger gnaws at my belly for I only have biscuits to eat. I stand warrior-like, a member of the Macdonald clan. We march to the beat of a drum, and the skirl of the bagpipes. I am ready.

Julia Jordan

I Remember

I remember the pain on Dad's face when he took me into the back shop and told me my three-year-old had suffered an accident and was in hospital.

Only the parents of disabled children, young or old, can know or simulate the anxiety and feelings of blame upon themselves for what has happened to their offspring. Those feelings never leave them, it hurts much more than you will ever know.

Maybe the children were born with a disability or maybe suffered an accident which maimed them for life, either way we blame ourselves.

Could we have prevented the incident before birth or the accident which caused the injury? We will never know which path we could have taken or even if the alternative had made a difference.

We must live with the knowledge that we can no longer change the circumstances, we must bear the pain, which is our burden.

Gwen Whitaker

Battle 1403

Church watches still where two Henry's fought
Plantagenet princes, each a bloodlust cause
Family ties weep, for the honour of a throne
Victory, scarred, a cousin's death to atone

Fields of silence, yet bleed a dynasties rage
Percy, Bolingbrook, violent sad battle wage
Arrows sped, Hotspur dismissed his helm
Tears in time, so a King kept his realm

Love mourns "for the souls of those who fell"
Peace reigns now upon a burning Royal hell
A monument blesses all who shed their lives
July gone, Shrewsbury's heart no longer cries.

Tina Bond

The Valley Of The Hollows

Alongside the waterfall
Tumbling down, icy and cold
We clambered up the steep path
Like the clansmen of old.

In distance, we hear the lonely wail
Of a piper at play
Above us grey clouds
On this wet blustery day.

Ahead, the path grows steeper
As we wearily trudge along
Back-packs grow heavy
As the birds trill their song.

Our holiday in the highlands
A memory, to treasure, and to keep
Climbing ever higher and higher
As we crave rest, and look forward to sleep.

At last, the legendary Lost Valley
Now partly covered in snow
Where the clan MacDonald fled in fear from their foe,
Back, in the Valley of Glencoe.

It seems surreal, now
As in those footsteps we follow
That desperate flight
Into the Valley of the Hollows.

As we stand in awe, all gazing
At this place, full, of past sorrows
Those haunting, voices, reach out from the past
In that secret place, the Valley of the Hollows.

Graham Peebles

Covid-19 WE ARE IN THE DANGER GROUP!

We went off to Spain although I had doubts
We'd heard of a virus that knocked people out
There's no problem yet in UK or Spain
To travel or not? No venture no gain.
WE ARE IN THE DANGER GROUP!

The hotel is fine we look over the sea
Our apartment is great with nice balcony
Free Wi-Fi a blessing as we would find later
As COVID took over we needed the data.
WE ARE IN THE DANGER GROUP!

There's boules pitch and darts down by the pool
And bingo at four, we'll win wine, that's so cool!
Rifles and archery just round the corner
For me, I'll just laze and then pop in the sauna.
WE ARE IN THE DANGER GROUP!

Hey ho you Blackie, the Pidgeon we've named
He comes every day I think he is tamed
He sits on our balcony puffing his chest
He bullies the others he knows he's the best.
WE ARE IN THE DANGER GROUP!

The virus has come we're told we must stay
But Gov.UK says we must go today
To stay or to go a quandary we're in the boarding cards
ready are these for the bin?
WE ARE IN THE DANGER GROUP!

Would you believe we're all set to go
When off goes a ping on my mobile you know
With trembling hands I look and just stare
At the message displayed yes it says Ryanair.
WE ARE IN THE DANGER GROUP!

They've cancelled us twice could this be a third
If I had wings I'd fly home like a bird!
It's only a message informing us that
A claim can be made to get money back!
WE ARE IN THE DANGER GROUP!

I'm writing this down before we depart
I know before leaving deep down in my heart
The road will be empty no cars to be seen
And so I am hoping to say 'I have been'
WE ARE IN THE DANGER GROUP!

Gwen Whitaker

The Shepherd

Spring is the time when we see lambs playing in the fields. They are enchanting to watch as they race around, bask in the sun, or sleep on their mother's backs. But spare a thought for the shepherd. Come rain or shine he must care for his flock, attend to other jobs on the farm, and may have another job to make ends meet. The luxury of having a shepherd whose job is simply to look after sheep is long gone. The modern world demands more.

The first thing to be said about being a shepherd is that it is hard. It's not just the sleepless nights at lambing time, when it is freezing cold and the rain horizontal, nor is it the physical work which is brutal at times; struggling to catch a sheep that doesn't want to be caught or to get a ewe to take to a lamb she has rejected just aren't fun. Sometimes you need an extra pair of hands. One lambing time, a Claverley farmer had caught a ewe in the field which was in trouble. The problem was he couldn't hold the ewe down. Just then the vicar arrived: heaven sent one may say. 'Come over here Vic and hold this ewe down for me,' the farmer shouted. The vicar duly lay on top of the sheep as ordered until a healthy pair of lambs were delivered.

So I've said that the long hours and the physical work aren't the hardest things. The worst is the emotional strain of looking after living creatures, of doing one's best for them at the expense, in many cases of one's self and family, of failing more than succeeding, the devastation of an animal dying, from whatever the cause. Of knowing that the buck always stops with you - that your skill and judgment will determine outcomes. There is no-one else to blame if something goes wrong.

This leads to dedication to the end. One shepherd's last words to his wife before he died were, 'I've fed the lambs.' That says it all. I haven't met a shepherd yet who didn't love his sheep beyond all reason. It is a mutual affection. Outsiders may think the job is done simply for the money. It is not. There are many ways of making more money, and much more easily than being a shepherd.

But there is a joy to the work, too. Sometimes it is appreciated best when you watch another shepherd at work. On this day I watch as a shepherd is doing a routine job, trimming sheep's hooves. His dog gathers the flock quietly, and once penned, the shepherd catches a sheep and tips it until it rests against his legs. He takes his shears to trim its hooves but the sheep moves uneasily. The dog edges forward to help but his work is done. The shepherd has the matter under control now and he settles the dog back down. And there they are; the three of them in perfect harmony, shepherd, sheep and dog.

So when you are out and about in the countryside this spring, enjoying watching the lambs in the fields, spare a thought for the shepherd, an anachronism in todays' society, living a life out of the public gaze, perhaps just as he wants it; him and his sheep.

Jane Smith

Monologue

The house where I grew up, 56, Buchanan Drive, Cambuslang was at the top of a hill. It had a view of the power station cooling towers, giant landmarks with clouds of water vapour hovering over them. I distinctly remember the front garden in particular with its rowan tree, the sturdy mountain ash in the middle of the lawn. Red berry clusters dangled from the branches in the autumn. Was it there one hot July that I stood and called out to passers-by, telling them it was my birthday and showing them my present, a blue handbag with a shoulder strap?

The greenhouse in the back garden smelled of tomatoes, earthy and smoky and so distinctive that if I catch a hint of their aromatic scent now I am transported right back to those early childhood days. I played with my younger sister, egging her on to do naughty things and getting her into trouble if I could. The coalhouse was piled up with hard black lumps of fossil fuel, their chiselled surfaces glinting in the light, exposed from their deep sedimentary sleep under the ground.Every day I walked backwards and forwards to school four times a day, plodding along staring at the pavement all the while. In the playground I linked arms with my friends and staggered about pretending to be drunk. Where did that idea come from?

Some days the class would go out on nature walks, studying beech nuts and berries and looking at trees. I hated the little glass bottles of milk with cream at the top. They were warmed by the radiator and given to us at playtime. Once, I was sick on my yellow plasticine. Then there was the time when, in spite of my shyness, I complained to the janitor about the state of the toilets.

Coming home at lunchtime one day I spotted the mobile grocer's van and climbed inside to spend my pocket money on a Milky Way. The advert claimed this was the sweet you could eat between meals. I discovered this to be untrue when I found myself unable to eat my dinner. I was in big trouble. Half a pound of stewing steak purchased from the butcher would feed five of us, parents, sister and grandmother . We called it 'dewing dake' after my sister's attempt to pronounce the words. We'd go down the road to get dewing dake at least once a week. In those days you shopped on a daily basis anyway. We had no fridge, just a pantry and a meat safe, a small wooden free-standing cupboard with doors and wire mesh to keep food cool and air circulating. Sometimes the dewing dake would go into the mincer, my grandmother squashing the chunks of raw meat into the metal mouth of the machine. The mince was extruded in strands. If we were still hungry after our meal we'd be given a 'jeely piece' or butter and sugar on toast. As the old song goes:

O ye cannae fling pieces oot a 20-storey flat 700 hungry weans will testify tae that. If it's butter, cheese or jeely, if the breid is plain or pan.
The odds against it reachin' earth are 99 tae wan.

Jeely Piece Song. Adam McNaughton.

Julia Jordan

I Remember When
From an old person's perspective

I remember a time when the sun was shining, and the birds were singing, and you could see all the birds in your garden with all the beautiful flowers that you had developed and grown.

I remember a time when children used to play in the streets with there sports balls whether that was cricket, football or even the old game of kerby. I remember a time when kids would play tag, bulldog and hide-and-seek.

I remember a time when elderly people would tell me that you could go out and not have to lock your doors because you didn't fear being broken into.

I remember I time when people would talk to each other without the use of social media or telephones to compensate for.

I remember a time when there were only five TV channels and if you wanted to change the channel you had to get up and change it yourself instead of relying upon a TV remote to do it for you.
I remember a time when you could go to the butchers and eat all sorts of types of meats.
I remember a time when you barely heard of crimes or people committing crimes in your area.

Peter James

The Key To It All

I found a key. That's where this story begins. But where, where did I find it? Aye, there's the rub. Taking a walk one afternoon, I followed the shortcut that leads through the village graveyard to my back garden. The autumn equinox had passed and the winter storms had begun to ravage the countryside. I found the world so dark and bleak.

Perhaps it was time to move back to the lights of the town? I had trodden this path many a time, a well beaten track with no surprises. Imagine my astonishment as I came upon the old crab apple tree tumbled across my way like a broken spine. It had been weighed down and crushed by the forces of wind and rain. I felt saddened to see this gnarled and ancient tree brought to ruin like this. Planted long ago to banish evil and connect those who had been buried with the afterlife it had stood the test of time until now.

To me, it had been a symbol of eternal youth, long life and renewal. What could this mean, the death of a tree? This moment turned out to be highly significant when I think of all that transpired afterwards. I approached to have a closer look. The trunk had split open revealing years of growth inside. But there was more to it. Within this deep rift I could make out an object immured within the wood itself. I eased my hand into the hollow and felt round the shape with my fingertips. It was cold and hard and deeply embedded under the bark. The living tissue of the tree had flowed around it, binding itself to it, engulfing it. After much effort scraping at it with makeshift tools I extracted it and in a moment of triumph a large key, tarnished and dulled with age fell onto the ground with a clangorous sound.

On further inspection I could make out an inscription along the shaft. By polishing the metal as best I could with my coat sleeve, I was able to decipher the following words: *Finders, keeper,'neath the church seeker.*

As I read the words aloud I could feel shivers running down my spine. A strange compelling energy and excitement was welling up inside me. What secret lay hidden beneath the church? I thrust the key into my pocket, rushed hurriedly past the lychgate into my garden and burst in through the back door. Once I had got my breath back and put the kettle on I sat down and laid the key thoughtfully on the table in front of me.

What would be the next stage of my journey of discovery, I wondered? What would I find in the damp and musty crypt of the church? A plan began to formulate itself in my mind. Tomorrow I must act.

Julia Jordan

Ghost of Bridgnorth

Magical light on the water soughs away,
Life, attainment, loss, redemption'
A Bird mocks my anxious thoughts,
Sardonic replete and oh so knowing.

Imperious, eternal, with reference to no-one,
Fast, faster, then restlessness gives way to somnolent calm,
I am the ghost that walks Bridgnorth,
Silent, mild, gliding along invisibly,
Destination unchecked neither sought nor wondered at.

That bell ends my reverie,
Such hope and light,
Waterside leafy branches gently part the waters,
Grown stark with waiting,
Half in their watery grave,
Pensive with time.

Sodden, depleted, silhouetted in the coming night,
A fiery surrender to a time stricken Styx,
I wonder... do footsteps continue and echo,
Across the ages through time,
An interface of the tawdry with touches of the sublime?

Ask not for whom the bells tolls...
That it may not burst its banks,
Contained, contiguous,
Where will it end,
This ordinator of time?

Karen Marley

Baschurch

I thought I'd go and visit Baschurch today
It's where King Arthur's buried or so they say
The sun shines so brightly upon this place
A radiance of glory that will grace my face.

I start my old car, the weather shall be fine
No rain about to halt this dream of mine
I shall cast my eyes upon his ground of rest
To the King I shall whisper, have I passed the test?

My car seems to know as where we should go
Up the M54, mirroring a steed in battle flow
Passing Wroxeter I think we should stop
Home of the King, I'll visit its shop.

Back on the road now, in search of our quest
On to Baschurch while the sun's at its best
No! Just seen a trickle on the window screen
I don't need this day to be a might have been.

The heavens open upon this country lane
I suppose, giving life to the earth this rain
Mud is flowing, an army blocking our path
Can't go forward and we can't go back.

Maybe it's him, and he's just trying to say
Now is not the time, come back another day
But maybe Merlin doesn't want to see
Where the King sleeps, Just let him be.

Tina Bond

47

~ Fantasy ~

Where the lost things are...

I want to find the place where the lost things are
Away from this world no matter how far

It could be close it could be here
But out of sight to all who peer

Somewhere that only I know
And nobody else knows where I go

Peace and silence, serene and calm
Cocooned within, and safe from harm

Where the lost things hide, then suddenly appear
Always where you've looked, and always near.

Julie Gorman

Leave the Weeds Alone

There are windows and doors and openings everywhere in other worlds. Small, large, alien, physical, mental….

Jennie felt a jolt like an electric shock not too strong but obvious. She was on her newly acquired council allotment getting rid of the top weedy overgrowth which had lain undisturbed for hundreds of years.

Surprisingly, she mentally verbalised, 'We're not weeds!'she heard a disembodied voice retort.

'Ow! You're hurting my ears! Stop pulling so hard!'

Jennie stood up and looked around and was startled to see very unfamiliar scenery laid out before her. She was now standing on a cliff looking out over a shallow purple sea with pink porpoises frolicking about in the distance. There were two blue moons hanging in the orange sky and a smiling little green and yellow man looking up at her.

He had the overwhelming look of a sunflower with wispy green tendrils growing out of his ears and a yellow halo of white petals around his yellow head. 'At last we meet, and not a moment too soon,' the two-foot stranger announced. 'You are standing on the ancient shallow Wondarappus Sea.'

Ann Bickley

The Symbol

Brenda Caraway gazed in horror at the symbol on her bank statement. It was no more than a plain circle with two tiny horns. Yet it seemed as though a modern-day Blind Pugh had presented her with the dreaded black spot!

And now with an uncanny feeling, Brenda was beginning to believe that she had, in fact, been cursed. For once her aura of unshakable self-belief and the ability to argue the toss on any subject under the sun was having serious consequences, as day by day, her confidence began to falter.

It had reached the point where she couldn't sleep at nights without seeing that wretched symbol in her dreams. Wherever she walked, that the damned symbol kept appearing, either daubed on posters within the city or scrawled on the walls of the ladies' loo. Even the novel she had ordered from the local library had been defaced on every other page with the dreaded, horned symbol. It had reached the stage that every tiny piece of misfortune which occurred in her life was attributed to that horned devil!

It had all began when she was invited to appear on a television show called the 'Great Debate' as a member of the audience. The topic was tailor-made for Brenda, 'Do witches have any real power?' It was an emotive subject and one that was sure to bring out the worst in argumentative people, especially righteous know it all's, who with a mixture of sarcasm and a talent for arguing their case. The subject made for great TV; usually at the expense of those who happened to have a different point of view.

The show's presenter called upon a quiet, shy looking young woman, who at a first glance looked like an

Amy Winehouse double, except that she wore classic, gothic clothing.

When Moon Raven made her contribution to the debate, Brenda laughed derisively and muttered loudly enough for everyone to hear. "Here we go again, another attention-seeking little wannabe, without any talent seeking to impress us all with her *magic* powers."

Moon Raven immediately turned and glared at Brenda balefully before she went on to explain how her chosen path within witchcraft had changed her life for the better.

After Moon Raven had given several examples of how her spells had effected changes within her own and other people's lives, Brenda in her usual fashion, bullied her way to the fore and proceeded with a mixture of ridicule and castigation, to belittle the young witch's beliefs. What made it worse was that Brenda had won the majority of the audience over to her side, and they too began to laugh derisively as Moon Raven aimed her baleful glare once more, at her tormentor.

'Why are you glaring at me like that?' Brenda scoffed, 'are you trying to frighten me with your useless magic. It doesn't really exist you know. So why don't you grow up, you silly little girl!'

In response, Moon Raven raised her left hand and extended her forefinger and little finger. Her eyes narrowed, and she mumbled softly while she pointed her horned god sign towards her tormentor. Like a flock of sheep, everyone in the audience including Brenda roared with laughter and derision.

Some time later in the foyer of the television studio, Brenda gave the young witch a smug grin as she walked past her. But quite calmly Moon Raven said, 'Three weeks from now you will come begging me to lift my curse; such is your blindness. But not before you have apologised and admitted that my powers of witchcraft are real. Until then enjoy the madness!'

Graham Peebles

The Gods

'Shall we have a little fun?'
Apollo whispered to the sun
'Turning the day into night
Artemis should give a fright'
For Zeus wants us to see
How far mere mortals flee
If Poseidon beats his drum
Watching ocean tides run,
Shall Ares tease from above
Or Aphrodite sprinkle love
Should Hestia say of afore?
'As flames they blazed upon our shore'
Will Athena aid one in flight?
May leave him alone to fight,
Can Dionysus ease such pain?
On waking he'll know in vain,
Hera, she frowns of Zeus at play
Makes him send those Gods away
Returns the world as it was before
The wife, she spoiled it all for more!

Tina Bond

Monokeros

Monokeros is my name. I stand unseen amongst the tapestry of leaves, hidden by the dark, damp branches of the forest. I remain elusive and solitary, a creature of mystical beauty.

My tread is so soft I barely crush the blades of grass as I run swiftly by, my hooves flashing in the sunlight. I gallop on picking up speed, faster and faster I go. No one can capture me alive unless by trickery or by the use of deadly arrows.

I can live for a thousand years. My strength is drawn from the deep and dark depths of my unconscious mind and settles in the part of me that is magic. I have the power to heal and the ability to counteract poisons. Just perceive the intensity of my nature and my invincibility. My body white as snow reflects the light and silver-blue blood courses through my veins. I appear in the day-lit world only fleetingly and often with reluctance.

Now as I look down I see the brown waters tumbling and rilling over the stones, it is murky with the rising sediment and unknown toxicity. Long gone are the wild Rainbow Trout and the Grayling, the freshwater mussels have vanished too. I steel myself and make the effort to bow down, bending my neck and piercing the cold water with my horn, the miraculous Alicorn.

Summoning all my powers I bring crystal clarity to the now sparkling ripples and my task is complete.
I turn to go back to that other world. As I told you at the beginning my name is Unicorn.

Julia Jordan

~ What's Going On ~

I'm on the Run

I'm on the run. Okay, I stole it, but it should have come to me years ago. The will clearly stated that it should go to the youngest member of the family. That was me. Nothing was said about being male or female, so my rotten cousin took it. He made such a fuss, I knew I wouldn't win, so I just kept quiet, awaited my chance and stole it from him.

When he went on holiday I broke in, wearing gloves, and went straight for it, getting in and out as quickly as possible and leaving no tell-tale clues.

I knew that this kind of thing could be disposed of quietly in France, so that's where I'm headed. I got my ticket in advance and with it safely in my innocent looking shopping bag, I was on my way.

I should get £5,000 for it, which I will keep, without too many pangs of conscience. Rotten cousin is well insured, so he won't lose out. He didn't like it anyway. I didn't like it either, but the money will come in very useful.

No one will suspect that I am the thief. Over the years I've studied crime and become a respected lawyer.

Kitt Ballinger

The Cardigan

Mark, Pam and Gillian were very quiet children. They had
to be. Their father was always on a short fuse; everything
irritated him. Children's voices were especially detested.
Children were just about okay as babies and toddlers, but
the advent of speaking was a great trial. Just a
contemptuous sneer was all he could muster with a
warning flash of, 'Don't come any closer. Keep away.
Don't say anything!

Mealtimes were difficult. He also had a
pathological dislike of noises at the table. No talking, no
eating noises, no 'American' ways of eating (chopping food
up first then putting the knife down and eating only with a
fork.)

There were consequences of disobedience. They
had witnessed a pudding bowl flying across the room and
strike Mark on the head when he had crunched a potato
crisp a bit too loudly and Pam when she had bitten into a
crisp green apple when a heavy jug was tossed her way.
Gillian's protestations of, 'I'm not going to eat those dead
caterpillars!' inside the over boiled cabbage met with her
dinner plate being upended on her curly blond hair.

One day a six-year-old Pam had accidentally
ripped her cardigan on a doorknob at school. She was
wetting herself at the possible consequences of home time
and the T. Rex waiting. So, she hatched a plan to switch the
blame to little Bernard Butterick her classmate at school.
He has teased her in the past, and she had heard of a
recent news story of a boy having a penknife. Perfect! She
thought. This would be the solution and to avoid his
wrath. She would say that Bernard had cut her cardigan
with a penknife.

'WHAT!!!??' roared her father and marched her down to the school the next day demanding an explanation. Poor, bewildered Bernard was interrogated by the headmaster, as was poor Pam, who soon confessed.

Needless to say father had to eat humble pie, which was not in his nature as he was a bully himself.

And Pam? What was her punishment? We can only conjecture... but it wouldn't be pleasant, would it?

Ann Bickley

Julia And Kate. A Cautionary Tale.

I know that I may seem like a nosy old cow, but really! I was making my way back home when who should I see, but Julia Price coming out of that posh looking house in Farthingdale Road. "Well... what on earth was she doing there?" I said to myself.

It was a good job she never noticed me, but I decided to hang around a bit. I mean if she's moving in those lofty circles, maybe I ought to know about it; after all she does like to get one over us mere mortals doesn't she, the snooty bitch.

I decided to take a little walk around the block, which took me all of a quarter of an hour. When I got about fifty yards along Farthingdale Road, she comes out as bold as brass and gives this tall fellah a great big kiss on the lips; right there on the doorstep... the slut!

Well, of all the nerve, I thought to myself, and a woman of *her* age having a toy boy on the side. I wonder what they'd think about that at the church coffee morning. I can see that I'm gonna have to do a little bit of digging, if only for poor Fred's sake; God rest his soul. Mind you if he knew what she was doing, he'd be spinning like a top in his coffin!

A week later, I waited to see if any of the church ladies had found anything out about Julia's going's on. If anyone was going to know anything it would be those pious load of so-and-so's.

Well, Julia came in and sat down by us complete with her cup of coffee and a plate of digestives. She sort of smiled at me and winked at Mavis Wright, the local gossip.

'And how's your week been Kate? Eventful? she asked.
Well... I just coloured up, didn't I, and could only manage a squeaky, stammering reply. 'No, n n n.... not really.'

I saw her eyebrows shoot up beyond her fringe, and that sly little smile playing about her lips, before she dropped her bombshell.

'Really? It appears that you saw me coming out of that large house in Farthingdale Road, and by all accounts saw me snogging a bloke passionately on the doorstep? You must have thought that I was a right brazen little hussy? But... for your information Kate, the owner of that house happens to be my younger step-brother Nick. I had just dropped off a present for his daughter; they've only just moved in, you see.

'As for the passionate snog on the doorstep; what a sordid little mind you must have? As a family, we've always been a little touchy-feely, and a tiny peck on the lips shouldn't suggest otherwise should it?'

Well... that put me firmly in my place didn't it; I don't know if I can face them all again. But I've learned a couple of lessons though; one, be careful who you trust, and two, from now on no matter what I see, I'll keep my big gob, shut!

Graham Peebles

The Golden Dragon — A sculpture by Dr Willard Wigan MBE

A golden dragon
Absolutely majestic
But microscopic

Julie Gorman

Tanka Poem

Bike

Only on my bike
Will I go for a long hike
Wiff waff air, no care
While I ride my bike today
I have nothing else to say

Peter James

The Islands Call

The water laps the shore
I hear the seagulls cry
They glide, they rise and soar
 Above the cliffs so high.

The island call is clear
The Inner Farne is bright
'Tis water that I fear
The distant lighthouse white.

The boat is standing ready
White horses I can see
The boatmen holding steady
The wind is from the lee.

I hear the captain's call
'We're off now to the Farnes'
I feel the rise and fall
More rough than on the Tarn.

With leeward wind behind
We sail with breakneck speed
I fear the rocks we find
The Captain pays no heed.

'Fear not' we hear him say
'I know these waters well
I sail this every day
'Tis just a tiny swell'.

Now as we near the rocks
The Captain calls 'I'll stop'
He must know of a dock
To tie up and jump off.

The anchor is unwound
And drops into the sea
With noisy clanging sound
It's happy to break free.

The Cameras are ready
Seals are now appearing
Their stares are quite heady
And oh so endearing.

'Ahoy' the Captain warns
'It's time to leave now
We're heading to windward
Wind strong to the bow'.

'Hold steady me beauty'
He talks to his boat
'I hold a great duty
To keep you afloat'.

We sail into harbour
We give a loud cheer
A day to remember
A memory so dear.

Gwen Whitaker

The Blank Card Drawer

Don't go into the drawer of blank cards. The ones I buy ahead of time. I buy them when they're cheap that day because I'm hopeless at remembering dates. The drawer provides a façade of organisation. It saves face with neighbours or an old aunt told me.

My daughter looked just like my grandmother. It consoled her; made her raise a wrinkled smile. I dived into the drawer sieving for the right card. I didn't know I'd bought so much ahead of time. Too far ahead. A card for 'Nanny on Her Birthday' that I had no one to give any more.

A card with a picture of scones and tea pots for Mother's Day. That one's no longer necessary in my card drawer. The woman who declared and scared everyone into thinking I look just like isn't here any more. I don't look anything like her. She was dark. I'm not dark enough. She was elegant. I'm stout. She just wanted to claim me. I won't have anyone to love me like that again. Where does all that love go?

I can't go back to that drawer any more. I might just tip the whole thing in the Recycling. Its tempting fate that there will be more useless cards to make me cry next time there's a new baby or a house move. More grief to be swallowed next time I delve. No more delving any more.

Dany Drummond

It Tolls For She

I lay on the forest floor, my stubbled chin propped up on folded arms. The brown pine-needles prickling my chest. Overhead the wind blew in the tops of the trees. A beautiful summer's day, the heat of the direct sun cooled by the gentle breeze.

In the distance I could see the church, prominent on the crest of the Hill. Cottages dotted round its perimeter, like sentries on guard. The hubbub of the wedding guests had quietened.
The bride's mother and bridesmaids were waiting outside the church. Then a white car, a Rolls-Royce or Bentley, drew up and stopped near the lych gate.
Sarah, stunning in a flowing white gown, was helped out of the car by her proud father. The bridesmaids fussed then in they all went.

I must have dozed and then woke with a shot. I could see the happy bride and groom, their parents, families and friends tumbling out of the church excitedly. The church bells pealed, echoing around the hills and vales. A celebration for my lost love. You could be happy.
I hope you are.

David Morgans

Poem from Central Mexico
Impressions of Tequisquiapan

Gigantic moon at five am
Bright stars
Humming bird sips from the fountain
Huge cacti flower
As the silent sun rises.

Dawn arrives with dogs barking
Lambs bleating
Sounds of wood chopping
We drink black tea and
Eat papaya, yoghurt and honey.

The town invites us
Cobbled streets, bicycles and horses
Crowds of holidaymakers
Cool inside the church
Statues veiled in purple.

In the heat again we hug the shade
Tasting goat's milk ice cream
The market bustles with life
We buy a cucumber, an orange and a loofah
No fried grasshoppers today.

Time to take a taxi back
Home safely and the washing's dried
Wining and dining the evening away
Before the light goes
And the sun sets.

Julia Jordan

~ Humour ~

From a Cats Perspective

My significant others interest me.
They may pay the mortgage, but it's my house!
I sit and stare at them all the time.
I can always outstare them mainly when I am hungry and
begin to press their buttons or when I want a cuddle.

I am a bit of a pest when I am not the centre of
attention. I left them a juicy mouse last week with the head
as well, the best crunchy bit! They must've enjoyed it as it
was soon gone. I do suffer from CAD or computer
attention deficit and NMS newspaper magazine syndrome.

I scratch inappropriately on my body or
furnishings, Paw prodding and bunting, meowing loudly
and pathetically. Cold wet nose in the middle of the night
only when they're sleeping deeply. Lying and drooping
myself over things they preoccupy themselves with, when
it should be me!

Pushing and grabbing things they want; pencils,
string, paper… and the pièce de résistance?
Vomiting up a hairball in a nearby shoe or slipper!
That certainly gets results.

Ann Bickley

Parrot

Parrot says, 'I talk'
I reply, 'Too much you fool !'
'Shut your beak you freak'
Birds do speak you know
To each other but not me especially you see.

David Sanders

Eggs for Sale

Eggs for sale
Nice wares, not for free
Honesty box
Don't take and flee
Why would you screw me?

David Sanders

Sammy the Snake

The day is warm, and I am happily hissing in Mrs Potts pit
Mrs Potts appears and says go home and hiss in your own
pit.
I do just that, and mommy appears and says
'I told you to hiss in Mrs Potts pit'
 I explained what had happened
She smiled, looked wistful and replied,
'How odd, I knew Mrs Potts when she had not got a pit to
hiss in, miserable cow!'

David Sanders

Trouble

There once was a kitten called Trouble
Who used to wee and leave a little puddle
No matter how we tried to make him go outside
He'd just stare at us, do it and then chuckle.

Julie Gorman

Eulogy For A Sandwich

Sammy the sandwich had a varied life
And many incarnations too
From a tiny seed put into the soil Where he grew, and he
grew, and he grew.

To an ear of corn blowing in the breeze
Until they came and cut him down
Then into a mill he was thrown
Where they pounded and ground him, around and
around.

He was mixed up for a little while
Then into an oven he was put
It was there they turned him into a loaf
And into thick slices he was cut.

They smothered him with butter, and laid upon him
Slices of onion and cheese
Then into someone's gob he went
And swift was poor Sammy's demise.

So spare a thought for our Sammy
As you sit there, tucking in
Remember our dear old Sammy
And all the places that he has been.

Graham Peebles

This Is The life!

It's dawned at last, my very own golden age
And I wish to be treated as a wise old sage
Eccentric I may be, but I brought you up
So it's my time now, and I'll fill life's cup.

No more I'm bothered by woes of work
Any responsibility I'll now proudly shirk
Roaming the countryside in a purple hat
You'll not moan if I take Merlin our cat.

Ready in his basket, we need little cash
Seeing all of England upon my bus pass
Don't try to call, I won't have my phone
You'll not see us, until we come home.

Where I shall hog the sky remote
You pay for it now, and so I'll gloat
Showing my friends your expensive wine
We'll all get drunk upon that red vine.

So my dears you'll come home and whine
I really won't mind the pleasure's all mine!!!!!!
Love mum xxx

Tina Bond

Two-Way Conversation

Scene; early 1960s; District Nurse on Mrs. Smith's doorstep.

'Hello Mrs. Smith. Is Brian at home?'

'Ees in bed. Wot y want im for?'

'I've been sent to take out his stitches.'

'They'm doin that at the 'ospital.'

'He should have gone back to the hospital last week, but he didn't attend.'

'Ee day say nuthin.'

'Well they have to come out today. Can you wake him up please?

Loud shout: 'Ger up Bri. Nus is eer.'

'Could you boil some water in a saucepan for me please: about a cup full.'

'If y want a cup of tay we ay got nun.'

'I need to boil my scissors and forceps.'

'Wot y want t d that for?'

'So I can take Brian's stitches out.'

'I'm gooin next door.'

'Well if you show me where you keep your saucepans I'll do it myself.'

'We ay got non. Er'l lend me ers next door.'

Mrs smith comes back and the instruments are put on to boil.

'Have you got today's newspaper please?'

'I'll goo next door. Wat y want t read the paper for?'

I couldn't tell her that in some places, the day's paper was the cleanest thing in the house. I put the paper on a chair, took off my uniform coat, folded it and placed it on the paper. Then I unfolded my apron and rolled up my sleeves. Mrs. Smith raised her eyebrows, sniffed and went into the kitchen.

No sign of Brian, so I opened the stairs door and called. Uneven treads were heard on the stairs, then the door opened and a tousled haired youth in a tight T-shirt and drainpipe trousers, shambled into the room and plonked himself down in an armchair.

This couldn't be right. He was far too young to have had varicose veins stripped.

'Will you pull your trouser leg up as high as it will go please,' I asked.

Mrs. Smith returns in alarm. 'E cor, they'm too tight.'

'We'll have to take them off then.'

'E cor. Ee's got no pants on.'

'They've got to come off. There will be sets of stitches from his ankle to his groin.'

Brian crosses his ankles and folds his arms, staring at me with a sickly grin on his face. I'd wasted enough time here. I grabbed his trouser legs and pulled so hard he was halfway out of the chair, holding onto his trouser waistband with one hand and trying to pull his tight top down with the other. I won! What a mess. He was filthy.

I got a clean, white cloth out of my bag and placed the sterilised instruments on it. Then, using the rapidly cooling water in the saucepan, added antiseptic and with gauze swabs gently cleaned the stitches. This was going to hurt.

Brian was totally distracted, attempting, unsuccessfully, to cover his manhood, so I worked quickly, then dabbed on more antiseptic and small dressings where needed.

'He can't put these trousers back on Mrs. Smith, they need a good wash. Can you get him some clean ones please.

'E ay got non.'

'Pyjama bottoms then?'

'E ay got non.'

'Next door?'

'Nah. Silly old cow wo lend us nuthin like that.'

'Well wrap him in a towel while you wash his trousers. Better still put them both in the bath.'

We ay got no 'ot water.'

Exasperated, I wrapped the used swabs in a sheet of newspaper and put it on the fire.

'Ea, wot y doin. I gotta tek that back next door.'

Oh, the joys of District Nursing!

Kitt Ballinger

My First Kiss

My first kiss
Was it all I expected?
Oh, yes and more
The thrill of his lips meeting mine for the very first time
The longed for dreamed of experience of a lifetime
The stars were sparkling
The fireworks exploding
And Catherine wheels spinning around inside my head
This is it I thought
I am in love forever
I have found him.
Inviting lips were yielding and melting, dry and nervous.
Not tongues just yet... later
This gentle first kiss was perfect
I will always love him
Everything has changed
Nothing would ever be the same again
I chucked him six months later.

Ann Bickley

Dear Brave Room-Mate To Be

I hope the advert finds you well.

I am putting this advert in the local paper to try and find a flatmate to share the cost of living with me due to the cost-of-living crisis right now.

I am an avid animal fan and have many in my flat. It is like an exotic freaky zoo. I have three spiders, two snakes (two of the spiders are deadly poisonous and one snake is as well), a cat called Psycho — sometimes he is a bit unhinged, a Rottweiler dog who is scared of the cat and a parrot who shouts out 'Wanker' to anyone who walks past. Last but not least a tortoise who punches anything and anyone who goes near him.

We are a friendly and funny bunch the minority of the time. The majority of the time we are a lively but unpredictable lot.

Our last flat mate was hospitalised due to being bitten by one of the spiders and spent two to three weeks in there. A few weeks after his hospitalisation he passed away from blood complications. Fluffy is always trying to bite things the tiny little rascal, bless him.

Our Rottweiler likes his belly rubbed and sometimes has tried to bite me, but this is not very often. Our cat hisses at anyone who goes to bed without giving him boiled ham but deep down he is lovely in his own special way.

Finally, the two snakes that are here can decimate a deer let alone a human but are rarely out of their cages.

The flat is a spacious area with lots to do and lots of animals to see and interact with.

Peter James

Pub Grub

I was stuck in a hole
Without a soul
Nor a proper goal

I was in a pub
Thinking, shall I get some grub?
I went to the bar
It felt so far

I pay for my meal
I say what a steal
Meal deal, for one
Thats a done deal
And that will get gone

I had my eye on a big fat pie
With chips and gravy
Or shall I go savoury
Hot and spice
Sounded rather nice

I chose a steak-n-kidney pie
I'm not sure why
I thought I'd give it a try

Knife and fork at the ready
And I'm feeling oozy and steady
My stomach rumbling and grumbling

I see the waiter coming over with food on the plate
Me and my stomach get into a right state

I demolish my food
It totally uplifts my mood
I finish my pie, I have to sigh

Still peckish
I feel like some cake
Oh, yes for goodness sake
Cheesecake galore and...
Of course I always want more
Cheese chocolate biscuit
So much to like
Not a lot to dislike
I finish my food
Once again it lifted up my mood

I am as full as I can be
I shall prove it
Just you wait and see
I can barely breathe
I can barely stand
I think I shall need a helping hand
On that note; I am now dying for a pee

Peter James

~ Everyday Life ~

Racing Mister Moon

The voices from the back, both shout
When he comes, back into sight
Another journey in our car
On a bright, moonlit night.

'Look there he goes, behind that tree
Can you see his face?
He's here again, that Mister Moon
And he wants another race.'

'Do you think he'll beat us home again?
Or shall we leave him far behind?'
We're racing Mister Moon, again
In a game of a different kind.

Moving quickly, along the roads
Climbing hills, and down again
Around the bends, the children shout
'We're racing Mister Moon, again.'

Now he's in front, behind that hill
Then he leaps, above a tree
'We're racing Mister Moon, again'
The children shout with glee.'

Quick! We've left him far behind'
Their squealing voices roar
'We're racing Mister Moon again
He won't beat us anymore.'

Another leap, now he's on our left
And now he's on our right
'He's a cheater is that Mister Moon
But we'll beat him home tonight.'

I pull the car onto our drive
Mister Moon's waiting overhead
'He's beat us again,' the children moan
As I tuck them into bed.

'Ah, never mind,' I smile
'We'll beat him tomorrow night
When we're racing Mister Moon again
Goodnight my dears, sleep tight.'

Graham Peebles

An Old Boot

I saw this boot somewhere last year
Yes, Tissington in Derbyshire
Dressing of the Wells was a great day out
With lots to see and talk about.

This boot was on a dry stone wall
Outside a cottage, quaint and small
 I think it was just one of eight
All marching towards the garden gate.

Each one was filled with lovely flowers
Smelling sweet in the April showers
'Tough as old boots', well-made from leather
Doing their job in all kinds of weather.

This boot had kept old Arthur's foot
Safe from harm, till the mine was shut
Peg—leg Arthur will never know
That his old boot would be on show.

It suddenly occurred to me
Now plant pots so expensive be
To look for boots beyond repair
And grow my favourite flowers in there.

Kitt Ballinger

Heavy Eyelid

Grief comes over me
Like a sleepy eyelid closing down
The ball of nausea in my stomach
Left one day

Just awareness of loss now
Unawareness of loss next
Awareness of loss then
Unawareness of loss

Opening and closing like an eyelid
Not leaving me
Part of me
Part of the rhythm of my body
Grief; it's within me

Dany Drummond

My Love My Mate

However fortunate the hour
My love can make it sweeter, sharing!
However much the years may teach
My love can make me wiser, caring!

No day so warm and sunny
But my love's arrival makes it brighter!
No moment quite so carefree
But my love's laughter makes it lighter!

The Earth is full of good things
Forests tall and oceans wide!
But how my world's enriched
When my love is by my side!

Gwen Whitaker

A Piece Of Art Which Is Special For Me

Before I get to the piece of art which is memorable to me, let me put it in context. When I was a child, I was often taken to my grandparents' house for afternoon tea. It was a treat with a variety of components.

The house was a modest 1930s detached house with a fairly small garden (large by modern-day standards) in which grandfather had created a vegetable patch beyond a trellis of roses. The afternoon would begin with a tour of the garden. I wondered at its neatness (our garden was much more haphazard) and the fact that all the vegetables were in neat rows. It was an inspiration to the young child I then was, aged between four and eight. Indeed, the garden could have been my chosen art work, but it is not.

After the tour of the garden we would go into the house and grandfather would perch me on his stool in front of his desk. He was an unusually tall man 6'- 2" or more, and the stool was so high he had to lift me onto it. A tin of pear drops was on the desk and one would be a real treat. Having settled me down, he would go to his glass-fronted book case, and take out a Lewis Carroll book. With enormous pleasure he would recite the Jabberwocky.

> 'Twas brillig, and the slithy toves
> Did gyre and gimble in the wabe;
> All mimsy were the borogoves,
> And the mome raths outgrabe.

It was beyond me, and I hated it, remembering no more than the first verse, but children then were not like children now, and I suffered in silence and hope I managed to respond as I should. I was saved from further torture by Granny calling, 'tea's ready'. If I struggled to appreciate the brilliance of Lewis Carroll, I had no difficulty appreciating the delicacy of Granny's tea; wafer-thin bread and butter, and bought apricot jam. Used as we were to half-inch slices of bread and home-made damson jam, Granny's teas were a work of art in themselves.

Then to the front room with grandfather, where he would tell me about all the artefacts he had brought back from India: a gold-topped table, a tiger skin, a piece of sandalwood with its delicious smell, brass bowls and plates, each one described with love. No longer was grandfather talking to me, he was talking to himself, reminiscing about twenty-five years of his life that no-one except a child had time to listen to. Any one of these artefacts (except the tiger skin which one of our dogs would later modify) were a piece of art in themselves, but as grandfather talked, my eye would be drawn to a picture hanging on the wall; a print, of course, but it made no odds. It was Holman Hunt's painting 'Light of the World,' a powerful image of Christ.

Did I appreciate that at the time? I doubt it. My focus was on the overgrown door and what was behind it. Did I analyse the painting's finer points and meaning, I did not. I just soaked it up and stored it in the deep recesses of my brain and from time to time I marvel at the beauty of this painting, the door with no handle on the outside, which we can only open from our side, and revisit in my memory that little house with its beautiful garden, and remember my grandparents with intense fondness.

Jane Smith

The End Is In Sight

What does it matter in the end
When we've traversed all life's bends
When we look back at all we've done
Did we spend more time happy or more time glum
Did we savour our lives in sips or waste it
Drank it down in a gulp not stopping to taste it
And now as we approach our final breath
Will we welcome or be fearful of death?

Julie Gorman

Last Person On Earth

I am here alone
No one to remember me
So, do I exist?

Julie Gorman

This Old Shoe

I have a shoe and it's not new
It's been here
It's been there
And it's been everywhere.

It slips on
It slips off
It goes here
And it goes there.

Through all pains
Through all gains
This shoe has been there
And has had its full share
Travelling anywhere.

Old and not new
Maybe needs stitching
Plus some glue
With the right tool and hand
This shoe could fit a brand-new brand.

Then this shoe
That is held up by glue
Could walk down the street
On some brand-new feet.

Peter James

Swan Song

Memories whisper, love's tear drops fall
One entwined soul drifts so sadly alone.
Sunrise no longer greets her life, her all
Time's shadows flow, as water unto stone.
Sorrowfully reminding of his dying call
Dreams echo of sleep, praying to atone.
The essence, of her fragile pure heart
Carelessly ripped, so needlessly apart.

Tina Bond

Just An Old Boot

Just an old boot, that's how they see you
Flung aside, with nothing left to do
Discarded on a pathway walked by many
Some may even toss you the odd penny.

Where have been old one, where have you been
Where have you left your hope and your dream
Tell me your stories for I'd love to know
Your trail in life' I'd be proud to go.

I see you among mountains many a path to follow
Exploring the ditches, dykes and green hollow
You've been a wanderer, a capturer of time
One day, I'll choose those steps to be mine.

Tina Bond

Country Eggs For Sale

Tis a pity it's shutting
Can't make a living anymore
After generations of farming toiling on the land
Sheep, cattle and poultry too
Geese, ducks and chickens
Powdered eggs during the war
Made a packet back then
The supermarkets killed the trade
Giant greedy business hands
Snatched a living from the smaller man
No room for you at all
We want it all and got it all
No choice now factory farming
No taste no goodness
It's gone
The country eggs for sale
At the bottom of the lane.

Ann Bickley

What A Time We Had.

'What's it like to ride a wave', I asked my Dad?
'Hmm just let me think, it car' be too bad'
'Shall I have go pops, what do you think?'
'Now you listen here, don't fall in that drink.'

'Can I have a ride on the donkey Dad?'
'Why would you do that? You'll make him sad'
I'll give him a pat then, and ask his name'
'Ar' that's much better it won't be shame.'

'There's a seagull chasing my brother Dad'
'Oh, suppose he's been feeding it the food he had'
He's really running pops, now he's fell in the sand'
'Bloody kids, I better go and give him a hand.'

'Can I have big red strawberry ice cream Dad?'
'Not now, and your mother's going to be mad'
It wasn't my fault he fell, and spoilt the whole day'
'Behave will you, the ambulance is on its way.'

'What's it like to stay in hospital? Just asking Dad?'
'I hope you never find out, for that you should be glad'
'Why's that nurse putting ice on my brothers head?'
'To put some sense into it, he should've listened to what I
said.'

'Can we come back to the seaside again our Dad?'
'Don't "our dad" me; you can be spiteful to that lad'
'I didn't tell him to go and feed that big bird pops'
'No! You just wanted us all to eat at the chip shops!'

Tina Bond

The Cancer's Curse

Cancer is a bitch
It takes your soul
Just like a witch
Right at the core
It is oh so, so sore.

If you only knew
That one in two
Will be part of the queue.

The cancer's cause, has no pause
It goes on and on and on without remorse
So let's stop the spread
Before half of us are all dead.

I want to create hope
However, I can't
As not many people will cope
It sucks your soul away
While your family beg you to stay.

Peter James

.

~ Biographies ~

Gwen Whitaker was born in the county of Durham, married with three grown up children, divorced and re-married. Her inspiration comes from her childhood while living in a huge area of coal mining; poetry and short stories emerging from personal experiences.

Graham Peebles is a Perton based, independent author and hails from the Black Country. He has published eight novels to date and is busy working on other books. Graham currently lives with his wife of fifty-two years, his daughter, two cats, and an ever-increasing collection of guitars, much to his wife's annoyance!

Jane Smith was born in Wolverhampton and has lived in the locality for most of her life. For the last fifteen years she has been researching the history of Worfield which continues to be a passion. She has written a number of books including, "Accidents in Wolverhampton in the Nineteenth Century," "A History of Worfield from Earliest Times," "Translations of the Manor Court Rolls of Worfield from 1327," "Margery the Mustard maker. Tales from in and around Worfield," and "Sadie. The Little Farm Dog," (a contemporary story of the loss of a farm).

Julia Jordan was born in Glasgow and after spending her early years there she moved down to the Midlands. She has always loved reading and literature, and she went on to study languages at Durham University. Trying her own hand at creative writing has made her appreciate more than ever the skills and craftsmanship of different authors.

Julie Gorman is a bit of a home bird, having never lived more than 10 miles away from her first childhood home. She is a singer-songwriter whose poetry often gets incorporated into her songs.

Ann Bickley was born in Shropshire and brought up in South Staffordshire. She is a retired school teacher; married with one daughter, a grandson and a granddaughter. She has passions for history, underdogs, cats and all of nature. She is a member of Perton Writers and is getting better with age.

Tina Bond lives and works locally.
She is a writer of poetry and short stories.

David Morgans was born in Wolverhampton and grew up in the Black Country. His interests include Wolverhampton Wanderers, rock music, and amateur Dramatics.

Kitt Ballinger has lived in Wolverhampton for most of her life. She has enjoyed writing light-hearted poems and stories since her teens. She qualified as a State Registered Nurse in 1963. She has written her mother's Family History and is currently writing her own Life Story.

Dany Drummond wrote a poem about her hard-working Nan, in her teenage years that she was quite pleased with. She then didn't write another thing or tell anyone, but kept her sparkling talent in the back of her mind.

One day in her 30s, she found the poem in the attic. It wasn't as brilliant as she remembered. Dany joined Perton Writers to meet other writers and to work on actually being as brilliant as her teenage self thought she was.

Karen Marley lives in Codsall, South Staffordshire, and has attended several courses in Creative Writing and Poetry over the years and has a BA in English. Karen read quite widely from childhood onwards and regards writing stories as one of her foremost interests. She has written several short stories and poetry and loves to let her imagination roam and her writing flow.

Peter James has lived in the Midlands all of his life and in regards to society's standards would be perceived as very young.

He is an avid fan of sport, but wished to explore the world of creative writing.

When it comes to his own writing, Peter enjoys the creativity, knowing that everyone's interpretation is different and that each person observe life from different angles.

Peter is awestruck by the imagination of writers like JK Rowling, George R. R Martin and J.R.R Tolkien.

David Sanders was born and brought up in Warwickshire and educated at Bishop Versey's grammer school. Fell in love with poetry due to a wonderful English master.

Travelled widely, now settled in Perton and with great joy, joined Perton Writers.

Acknowledgements:

Thank you to all the members of Perton Writers for your most valuable contributions. You really are a wonderful group of talented people.

Graham Peebles

Printed in Great Britain
by Amazon